The Boy Who Spoke Chimp

by JANE YOLEN

illustrated by David Wiesner

Alfred A. Knopf / New York

This is a Borzoi Book
Published by Alfred A. Knopf, Inc.

10 9 8 7 6 5 4 3 2 1

Library of Congress Cataloging in Publication Data
Yolen, Jane H
The boy who spoke chimp. (Capers)
Summary: Stranded in the coastal mountains
following a devastating California earthquake,
a 12-year-old boy and the chimpanzee he rescues
from a wrecked van communicate through sign language
as they struggle to survive.
[1. Chimpanzees—Fiction. 2. Survival—Fiction.
3. Earthquakes—Fiction] I. Title.   II. Series.
PZ7.Y78Bp [Fic] 79–27259
ISBN 0–394–94467 lib. bdg.
ISBN 0–394–84467–X

Friday's vocabulary illustrations by Mimi Harrison

For Heidi,
who would like to speak to chimps,
and the I.M.:
Ann, JeanneMarie and LeeAnn

Contents

THE BOY WHO SPOKE CHIMP

1/ The Mirror Hero

"Absolutely not," Kriss heard his father's deep voice rumble through the wall. He got out of bed quickly and opened his bedroom door a crack to listen. He knew that his father must be saying something about him. His parents never argued unless the subject was Kriss.

"He positively cannot go camping by himself. Not yet. He's not ready. Maybe later. You know that kid's a disaster in the woods. He gets poison ivy by looking at it. Sunstroke by being out in the daylight. He stumbles over every branch and twig around.

He just doesn't use his eyes. Always has his nose in a book, that's what's wrong. At his age, I had been up and down . . ."

". . . the coast by myself three times," Kriss finished his father's sentence in a whisper. He had heard it all before. He went back to his bed carefully, sat down, and looked out of the window. Without his glasses, he could only see a bright blur. But he could still tell that it was going to be another beautiful summer day. Somehow the thought depressed him. Nothing ever changed in L.A.—not even the seasons.

He had hoped for a change when they moved to the West. Three years ago, West Los Angeles had fallen into the sea—one of the earthquakes that was always predicted and never seemed to happen. After the clean-up, a building boom had started. His father, a master mason, had moved the family from Brooklyn to a suburb of L.A. where the big jobs and the government money was. His mother, who, like Kriss, had been born and brought up in Brooklyn, had argued against the move. "What if there's another earthquake?" she asked every time a rain cloud dared cross the bright blue California sky. Another earthquake—that was her only worry. But there hadn't been another one. Kriss' father said there never would be. He had been born on the West Coast, and he *knew*.

Kriss thought that the move back to his father's old home would change things. Now his father would let Kriss try outdoor sports like camping and hiking. Kriss had read all about the California woods. He felt he was ready. But his father did not. He only said that Kriss was "a walking woodland disaster."

But this week, Kriss promised himself, things *would* be different. He was planning to take matters into his own hands. He was supposed to be going up to his grandmother's house near the Big Sur mountains. With his

sleeping bag and backpack, he'd be camping out in her back yard. Twelve years old and he still had to tent close to his Nanny's house! His father called it "learning to make the grade," but to Kriss it felt like kindergarten.

Kriss picked up his glasses from the bed-side table and put them on. The room came into focus, and he glanced guiltily at the one messy corner where he had thrown his camping gear in the middle of the night. His plan was to pack quickly and be on his way before his father came in to check out his backpack or his mother came in with her usual box of Kleenex. He was going to pretend to go by bus to his grandmother's, leaving his parents a note about an early start. But instead of going all the way by bus, he planned to go only as far as Soledad. He would hike and camp the rest of the way. *By himself.* Even if he messed things up, he would probably reach his grandmother's house in about four days. By that time everyone would be good and worried. And then he'd walk in the door looking tanned and fit and say casually, "Any calls?" He'd get a hero's welcome.

Kriss stood and stretched, scratching his stomach under his pajama top. Then he went over to the mirror and spoke to his reflection. "Of course you don't look like a hero," he said seriously. "Not yet. Maybe later."

He smiled, and the glasses slid down the short bridge of his nose. He pushed them back without thinking and went to the corner where his gear was piled. Putting things into the pack, heavy stuff on the bottom, light on top, just as his father had taught him, Kriss checked off each item on a master list:

Sleeping bag

Compass (of course)

A map of Northern California

A booklet about plants that are safe to eat

Six granola bars and some packets of dried apricots and dried apples (just in case)

A plastic bottle filled with water

A box of Band-Aids, bottle of Mercurochrome (iodine, his mother's favorite, stung)

One clean pair of underpants, socks

Toothbrush, toothpaste

Six-bladed pocketknife (The one time he had tried to use it, he had broken a fingernail opening it and his father had had to help. But he was sure he could get it open in an emergency, nails or no nails)

A ball of string

Three pencils, sharpened, and a notebook

$11.23 (his life's savings except for the $2 bill
he refused to break)

Six books for reading, *Robinson Crusoe* for
advice

Kriss got dressed, smiling slightly, and slipped the list into his pocket along with a pack of Kleenex. "For you, Mom," he whispered. He was about to put on his backpack when he remembered.

"The note," he said out loud. "I have to leave them a note." He thought a minute, then went to his desk and wrote in his careful handwriting: *I'm going to Nanny's early. Don't worry.*

He made his bed with the hospital corners that his mother liked so much, and put the note in the middle where it couldn't be missed. Then he picked up the note again and underlined *Don't worry* thoughtfully. The paper ripped slightly.

Frowning, Kriss put the note back on the bed and stood up. As he turned, he caught another glimpse of himself in the mirror. He took off his glasses and put them into his shirt pocket, smoothed the cowlick at the back of his head, and lifted his pack.

"Well, sort of like a hero," he said at last, squinting at himself. Without his glasses, all he could see was a skinny blur.

He sneaked past the kitchen and out of the house. He could hear his father at the breakfast table. "I know he's a good kid. A bright kid. And I *do* love him for what he is. But what he *isn't* is a woodsman. He can't be out there alone. Not yet. Let him out alone, and he'd probably be eaten by bears."

2/ The Lab Lugger

At the bus station, Kriss realized he didn't have enough money for a ticket. Usually his mother bought it.

"So much for planning ahead," Kriss thought gloomily. He hated the idea of going back to the house, where his father would probably laugh at him. He'd rather be eaten by those bears.

Squaring his shoulders, Kriss walked out into the sunshine, down to the corner, and stuck out his thumb. The very first car stopped before he could change his mind.

"We're going north," called out the driver,

a teenager. "Up 101 aways. Good enough?" The front seat held two others his age. They grinned at Kriss, looking friendly.

Kriss nodded, afraid to test out his voice. He was sure it would squeak a "No" at them. His mother had always warned him against hitching and, even though the kids in his class did it all the time, he had never dared try. ("But a hero has to try anything," Kriss reminded himself silently.) He crawled into the back seat, forgetting to take off his pack. By the time the car started up again, he was too embarrassed to struggle out of it. He would rather be uncomfortable than admit he was new at this sort of thing.

About an hour out, they let him off and squealed away to the east, waving good-bye. It was the closest they had gotten to a conversation with him the whole time.

Kriss looked up and down the highway. L.A. was a long way off. "I guess I have to go forward," he mumbled. In a way he was relieved.

He stuck out his thumb again.

Five rides and six hours later, his back aching from the pack, Kriss felt like a pro. He had ridden with a family; with two salesmen; with a group of women who had stopped for him because, as they said, they couldn't tell if he

was a boy or a girl; and with a fast-talking gum-chewer in a big trailer truck. The truck had been the best ride, barreling along the highway. The driver had gone on and on about the joys of the road. No one had asked Kriss hard questions and, after the first ride, he had remembered to take off his backpack and put it on the seat by his side.

Waving to the truck driver as he disappeared around a bend, Kriss took the map from his pack. He leaned against a sign that showed the Route 1 fork. The map said Route 1 ran along the coastline. Kriss lifted his head and sniffed the air. He could almost smell the ocean.

He thought about camping at night with the sound of the surf pounding below him. He would sleep under a twisted cypress tree. They were supposed to grow nearby. Maybe he'd hear the bark of sea lions defending their territory. Kriss put the map back, raised his pack, and trotted to the turnoff. The fog had cleared, and he knew it was going to be a wonderful day.

An hour later, Kriss was still waiting for a ride. Few cars passed along the coast road. The ones that did were mostly chock-full of tourists and suitcases. They all had out-of-state licenses. None of them even slowed down. Dejected, Kriss sat by the side of the road and took out a book. He was about to start reading when a white van pulled up.

"Hey kid, want a ride?" the bearded driver shouted out of the window. "Better hop in. Not many cars come along here."

Kriss jumped up and jammed the book into his pack. "Sure," he said. "You going up the coast?"

"Slow and steady," called the man. "The scenic route." He smiled, though just his bottom teeth showed because of the moustache.

Kriss smiled back and got in. He took off

his pack and put it between them. Then, hearing a chattering noise from the rear of the van, he turned to look.

"Wow!" he gasped. In the back of the van were several large cartons and a cage with two small chimpanzees. They were hooting and pointing at him.

"Okay, shut up back there," the driver called out. He turned in his seat and made a chopping motion at the chimps with his hand. All at once the animals were still.

"Are you from a circus?" Kriss asked. "Or the movies?" His eyes were wide.

The man laughed. "None of the above. What I am is a truck driver. Name's Ed. These are two of the talking chimps from the UCLA Language Lab. I'm just bringing them up to Berkeley for more testing."

"They can talk?" Kriss asked.

"Well, not really *talk*. They can sort of make words with their hands. You know, like a deaf guy. But monkey-see-monkey-do as

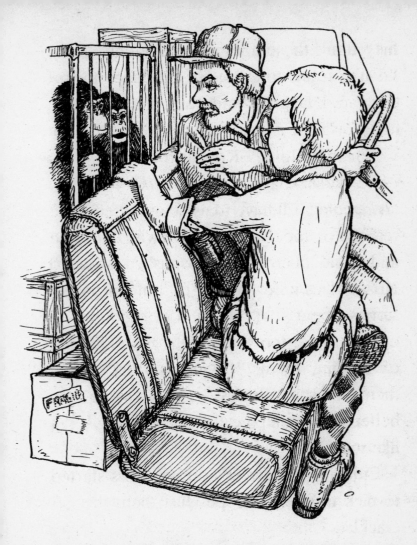

they say. Still, they sure know what *shut up*
means." He chopped down with his hand
again. "Those professors at UCLA, though,

they think these apes can really talk. *Talk!* I'd like to see one pledge allegiance to the flag." Ed laughed and Kriss laughed with him.

"Or tell a joke," Kriss said timidly.

Ed laughed again. "Say, I *like* you, kid. *'Tell a joke!'* I'll have to use that myself." He reached on top of his CB radio with one hand and found an envelope. He pushed it toward Kriss. "This here's a copy of some magazine stories about the chimps. I'm supposed to deliver these, too. You might get a kick out of reading them. If you can understand them, that is. Professors can't write any better than chimps can talk. *'Tell a joke!'* I like that."

Enjoying the driver's praise, Kriss started to pick up the envelope. Just then, the CB crackled.

"I'll get it," Ed said. "It's probably for me." He laughed at his own joke as he picked up the mike.

"Ranger Rick calling all my buddies," came a voice from the box. "Get me in good, you haulers. There's bad word coming."

Ed flicked a switch and spoke into his mike. "This is Lab Lugger, good buddy. I'm onto you loud and clear." The line crackled with other call-ins for a few seconds. Kriss heard names like Tugboat Annie, Easy Rider, Shotgun Shogun, and Jungle Jimmy.

Then Ranger Rick came back on the air. "There's word out of the seismo labs that another big quake is coming. Bigger than big. Gonna make West L.A.'s drop into the sea look like a kiddy slide. Huuuu-mungus. Get off the coast roads. Get off the thruways. Head for the high ground. I repeat, good buddies, head for the high ground. Grand-daddy quake's a-coming. The big one is on the way."

3/ A Little Tremblor

Kriss grabbed his pack and hugged it in front of him.

Ed the driver laughed out loud. "Don't worry, kid. They send out that warning every couple of months. Old Ranger Rick's a bit of a nut on the subject. See, his old lady was in West L.A. when it slid over the edge. And those guys at the seismo labs, why they about have heart failure every time someone walks too heavy by one of their machines. Up here we never get anything more than a few shakes. You know, what the scientists call tremblors."

"Tremors," Kriss corrected quietly, but the driver didn't seem to notice.

"Just little bitty tremblors," the driver continued. "Nothing to be scared of."

"Are you . . ." Kriss's voice squeaked. "Are you sure?"

"Am I sure?" Ed half turned around in his seat and made a quick movement with his hand, drawing his lips well back from his teeth and growling loudly at the monkeys. The chimps began screaming and jumping up and down in their cage. Ed turned back toward the road. *"But can they tell jokes?"* He beat one hand on the steering wheel and laughed.

Kriss began to relax. He put the pack on the seat again.

Just then the van began to shimmy.

"Holy hosannah," Ed shouted, grabbing onto the wheel with both hands.

Kriss was so scared he was sure he was going to be sick. For a moment it seemed as if the truck would break apart. Then just as suddenly, the trembling stopped.

Ed sighed heavily. Then he smiled, his teeth tight together. "See what I mean," he said. "Just one of them little tremblors. I've ridden them out before. There's nothing to worry . . ."

And then the big quake hit them, rolling and twisting and buckling the earth. Kriss thought it looked as if a giant hand had picked up the road and was flicking it at them like a large gray beach towel. One minute the van was riding along, and the next it was over on its side. Kriss never saw what happened in-between. He fell against his pack, which crashed against Ed. Kriss's glasses slid off his nose, and all the world blurred.

For a long moment he lay still, afraid to move, as if shifting his weight might start another tremor. Underneath him, Ed was silent. The CB crackled with static, but no words came out. Then from the back of the van came a crying, a soft *hoo-hoo*ing, like an infant longing for comfort. It went on and on.

At first Kriss thought he was the one crying. He certainly felt like it. But the sound came from the rear of the truck. He braced himself against the dashboard and tried to peer over the seat. He could see nothing in the back and realized his glasses had fallen off. He fumbled along the floor until he found them, up against the gas pedal. One of the frames was cracked. Putting them on,

Kriss looked again. The cage with the chimps was on its side, tumbled in with the cartons. He could see something slippery on the side of the van where the cages lay. The smell was awful.

The crying seemed to come from the cage. The two young chimps were holding on to one another tightly and moaning.

Kriss suddenly began to whimper along with them. They must have heard him, because the larger of the two held out its hand to Kriss.

Kriss snuffled once and wiped his nose with the back of his hand. Then he called out in a cracking voice, "Please don't cry. I'm coming to help." Under his breath, he added, "I hope."

He pulled himself over to the steering wheel and tried to wake Ed. But there was blood coming from the driver's nose, and the window where his head lay was smashed. He did not seem to be breathing.

"Oh, no!" Kriss caught his lower lip with his teeth and bit down. The pain cleared his head. He scrambled over the seat and into the back of the van. If the driver—he could not think of him as "Ed" any more—if the driver was dead, Kriss did not want to be anywhere near him. The very thought made him start to shake. He had never even *seen* a dead person before.

The young chimps began to *hoo-hoo* again, and the CB static cleared for a moment. Kriss heard ". . . repeat, get to high . . ."

Kriss looked at the radio. Then he sighed. Turning to the chimps, he spoke slowly and clearly. "High ground. We'd better get to high ground."

The cage was fastened with a combination of latches and bolts. The wire mesh was too fine for the chimps to get their fingers through to the locks, but Kriss opened the door easily. The chimps slowly crept out. They came over and touched him tentatively.

Kriss patted them back. Then he clenched his teeth and returned to the front seat, leaned over, careful not to touch the driver, and grabbed his pack. He pulled it over in three huge yanks. As an afterthought, he picked the envelope off the dashboard.

Then he spoke once more to the chimps. "That was the easy part," he said. "Now comes the hard part." His voice seemed to echo in the van.

At his voice, the chimps dropped hands. The larger one climbed over the cartons and fiddled for a minute with the rear door of the van. The door opened and the chimp turned toward Kriss, motioning with its hand palm up.

"Okay," said Kriss. The other chimp clapped its hands. They clambered over the boxes together, Kriss pulling his pack after them, and went out the open door.

The air was sweeter and fresher than anything Kriss had ever smelled.

4/ The Big One

Kriss could still feel small tremors underfoot. He looked around quickly. Up ahead of the van were two cars, both overturned. The nearest one was burning, sending oily smoke into the bright blue sky. Behind the van, the road was empty as far as he could see.

The road! That was a laugh. It was a jumbled mass of tar-colored building blocks. Kriss sucked in his breath at the sight and shook his head.

From afar he could hear the growl of the ocean as it attacked an unseen shore. Underneath him the earth seemed to answer the water, growl for growl. The chimps were already scampering up the side of the road, up a slope. Kriss thought he'd better go with them. Even if they had been born in a laboratory, they probably knew more about living in the wild than he did.

Kriss shouldered his pack and tried not to think about the people left in the cars. If he thought too hard, he would begin to cry. He was afraid to start crying. He might never be able to stop. Kriss sucked in his breath and followed the monkeys up the hill.

Kriss was breathing hard by the time he reached the top. Under some pines, he looked back down to the road. The van and the two small cars looked like a disaster picture on the news. But this was no show, Kriss reminded himself. This was real life. And real people were trapped inside those cars. He let his pack drop to the ground and shoved his glasses back on his nose, cracking the frames even more. Some of the people in the cars, he thought fearfully, might still be alive. And what kind of a hero would he be if he didn't at least *try* to help?

He took another great gulp of air, left his pack, and raced down the hill. He ran as fast as he could. The chimps chattered behind him, but he did not look back.

The ground around the van was still. The tremors had stopped for the moment. Kriss crawled in through the rear door and listened. There were no sounds. Slowly he made his way across the cartons, blocking his nose against the smell.

He gulped once, then climbed over the seat. The driver had not moved. Kriss could not bear to touch him, but he did. He picked up the driver's hand, trying to find a pulse. The hand was limp. Kriss dropped it and, without noticing, wiped his own hand across the front of his shirt. He bit his lip again, and just then he heard a voice come over the CB radio. It frightened him so, he let out a cry.

". . . Ranger Rick. This is Ranger Rick. That one measured 7.0 on the scale. They say there's another one coming. Phone lines down. Electric and water out. I'll stay on as long as I can. Get to the high ground. Repeat. A bigger one coming. This is Ranger Rick." The message began again.

Kriss scrambled out of the van as fast as he could. He could feel small tremors again. "Tremblors," he remembered the driver had said. Ed had said. He ought to remember Ed's name. A sort of memorial. His teeth began to chatter and his glasses started to dance on the bridge of his nose. He ran off the road and started up the grassy shoulder.

Then the big quake hit, throwing him to the ground. He grabbed his glasses with one hand. The frame cracked almost in two. Holding them onto his nose, he watched as a great jagged mouth opened up on the road below him. It followed the coastline. First the two smaller cars seemed to hang in space. Then they disappeared into the mouth. The crack raced on its jagged course toward the van.

Kriss got to his knees and crawled further up the hillside, clawing at holds in the grass and chaparral. His glasses dangled from one ear but somehow did not fall off. Behind him he heard a roar and dared a look back. The van seemed to straighten up for a moment and then, as if in a slow-motion movie, it slid into the crack. The crack closed over the van, opened up again, and sped along its way.

Kriss fell on his face and held on to the grass, screaming. When he finally stopped for a breath, he realized that his scream was the only sound he could hear. The roar of the quake was gone. The van was gone. The road was gone. No birds sang.

Then, as if to fill up the silence, he suddenly heard, closer than it had been

before, the voice of the ocean. It was beating and beating upon a new and very different shore.

Kriss looked up. Overhead, a solitary seabird sailed across the sky.

He stood, tears running down his cheeks. The earth no longer moved, so he walked up the side of the hill, adjusting his broken glasses. When he got to the top, he saw that the envelope lay where he had dropped it. But the chimps and his backpack—sleeping bag and all—were gone.

5/ Kriss on His Own

Night was a long time coming. Kriss checked the area over and over for signs of the two chimps and his pack. But he could find no trace of them. It was as if they had never been.

He looked in his pockets and came up with a pack of gum, the master list, fifteen cents—a dime and five pennies—and the pack of Kleenex. He chewed the gum slowly, piece by piece, until every single piece lost its flavor. Then he rolled some of the chewed gum around the frame of his glasses to hold them together. He made a face while doing it, but it worked.

The gum seemed to make him hungrier than before. He began to search the under-brush for berries, never going out of sight of the open hillside. Without a compass, it would be too easy to get lost. For all his reading, Kriss realized he did *not* know the woods. His father was right. And there might really be bears—here.

He found several bushes with red berries, waxy-looking and hard. He did not know what they were, and without his plant book-let he was afraid to try one.

"All I need now is a stomachache," he said out loud. He liked the sound of his own voice. Then he chuckled, remembering the Kleenex he had brought. "Be prepared!" he said. Then he shouted it: "BE PRE-PARED!" There was an echo but no answer.

Kriss bent over and picked a stalk with

purple bell-like flowers. He put it in the buttonhole of his shirt and let it tickle his chin. Finally, he flopped down under a small pine and picked up a handful of pine needles. He let them trickle through his fingers and made up his mind to think about nothing. The air was bright and heavily scented with pine and flowers. He felt exhausted and put his head on his arms. But although he closed his eyes and remembered home, he could not sleep.

Suddenly the hillside was alive again with sounds. Croaks and calls, squawks and growls. Kriss opened his eyes and turned over onto his back. Above the ocean he could see several large birds wheeling and diving. They looked like cormorants or pelicans. And from the trees in the clearing, little birds were singing again. He saw flashes of blue, yellow, and brown. A tiny humming-bird flew right by his face, a tiny splash of red. Kriss wished it could delight him, but all he felt was an overall fear. Fear of another quake, fear of the road, fear of never getting home.

He sat up again, putting his back to the tree. He was still sitting that way an hour later when the evening fog began to roll in. The fog gave him some measure of relief. He figured that if he couldn't see anything, nothing could see him. He closed his eyes, tasted the salt of fog and tears on his mouth, and fell asleep.

When he woke again, it was dawn. He was lying on his side. A pine needle was tickling his nose, and little pebbles dug into his side. His back ached, he was stiff, and something warm lay curled up beside him.

Fearfully, Kriss opened his eyes. The two chimps had come back. One was cuddled against his chest for warmth, its thumb in its mouth. The other, the larger of the two, had its arms around Kriss's pack. It was fast asleep and snoring lightly.

6/ Talking Chimp

Kriss opened his mouth, but no words came out. He was afraid to breathe. Carefully, he felt around and found his glasses. He put them on, then reached over and snagged a finger around the backpack's strap. As he slowly pulled it toward him, the littlest chimp woke.

In one fluid movement, it was up on its feet, chattering. Then it rolled over on its back. With its feet in the air, it began tickling itself with one finger on its own belly. It stopped a moment, looked at Kriss, then repeated the tickling.

It was so silly-looking that Kriss laughed out loud. At the sound of Kriss's voice, the chimp scampered away.

Kriss sat up, put his hands over his mouth, and stared. But behind the hand, his mouth was still smiling.

The little chimp edged back, watching Kriss all the time. It moved over to stand by the bigger monkey, who was now awake and staring.

Kriss put his hands out to them and crooned softly: "Come on. Come here. Look, see I won't hurt you." He spoke the same phrases over and over until they became a kind of song.

The bigger chimp sat up, its hands in front of its mouth, flapping its pink fingers in a peculiar way. But the little chimp gave a soft grunt and flung itself at Kriss, right into his arms. Kriss almost fell over, but he held on. The chimp nestled into his arms like a baby. It looked up at him, its dark, liquid eyes staring and its funny squashed nose wrinkling. Kriss hugged it gently. The chimp put its hand to its mouth and made a big fat kiss in the middle of its own palm.

"Okay, kiss," said Kriss, and he kissed the top of the chimp's head. It smelled like a wet dog. Its hair was thick and rough. "Phew," Kriss complained softly, "you sure are no movie star."

He put the little chimp down, but it would not leave his side. Kriss looked over at the big chimp and saw it was starting to go through his pack.

"Hey, leave that alone," he shouted. "Bad. Bad monkey." He jumped up and moved toward the chimp, waving his arms. It backed away, dragging the pack, and giving Kriss a strange grin. Its lips were well drawn back and its teeth showed.

Kriss began to chase the chimp, up and down in front of the trees. The little chimp joined in the chase, too, sometimes helping

Kriss, sometimes helping the bigger chimp.
Soon a kind of game developed. The monkeys kept just out of Kriss's reach, taking to
the trees with the pack to avoid him. But it
was no game to Kriss. Everything he owned
was in the pack.

At last, Kriss flopped down on the ground,
winded. He put his head in his hands and he
groaned out loud. "Dad was right. I *am* a

disaster, a natural disaster," he muttered. "Without bears!"

Just then, he felt a hand on his arm and looked up. The big chimp touched him, left the pack, and backed off. Then it squatted and watched Kriss's reaction.

Kriss picked up the pack and held onto it for a minute until he realized the chimp was not going to take it away again. Then he set the pack down and searched through it, coming up with a granola bar. He unwrapped it and started to eat. The little chimp moved closer, making a pleading *hoo-hoo* noise. Kriss looked down at the bar, then up again at the chimp.

"Oh, all right," he said at last, and found two more bars. He threw them to the chimps. "Eat up," he said, putting the bar to his mouth and taking an exaggerated bite. "Go on, eat," he urged, his mouth full.

The little chimp motioned to its mouth with its right hand. The big chimp tore the wrappers off both bars and shared with the little chimp. They ate, never taking their eyes off Kriss. When they finished, they motioned to their mouths again.

"That's it for now," Kriss said. "Or we may have problems later on. Who knows how long it's going to take to get back to L.A."

The chimps looked at him for a moment longer, then started chasing one another in quick little rushes. First one would run off and the other would follow, then they would switch places. Their play took them closer and closer to the trees. Finally they disappeared into the woods.

"That's the last I'll see of them," Kriss predicted. "And good riddance." But he suddenly felt very alone and very scared. He took out his compass and his map and tried to find out where he was. He remembered the turnoff and the sign for Route 1. But he had no idea how far up the road the van had come before the earthquake. He checked the compass. If he wanted to get to Los Angeles, he had to go south. He could follow the road, but was there a faster way? And what if there was another quake? Shouldn't he keep to the mountains? Of course, in the woods there was always the possibility of bears. Real bears. He remembered his father's words.

The thought of his father, suddenly so far away, maybe even hurt in the quake, brought tears to his eyes. He took off his glasses, careful not to disturb the chewing gum that held the frames together, and wiped his eyes. He needed a Kleenex, and once he had it, he thought of his mother. His eyes got tearier.

"No crying," he warned himself. "Heroes don't cry!" He rubbed his eyes and snuffled. Then he straightened up, put his glasses back on, and cleared his throat.

A sudden noise made him wheel around fearfully.

The two chimps came out of the woods,

their arms full of stuff. Walking on their hind legs, they waddled with a funny side-to-side motion. They came over to him and put the stuff down at his feet. Then they made the eating motion with their hands before digging into their treasures.

Kriss squatted down and looked at the piles. He recognized wild pears and several kinds of berries. He did not know if the berries were safe to eat. There were two small speckled eggs, which the chimps grabbed and bit into, slurping the insides eagerly. The little chimp opened its hand. In its palm lay several very dead insects. It offered them to Kriss.

"No thanks," he said.

The chimp licked its palm clean of the bugs. Kriss felt his stomach turn. He'd never get *that* hungry. But he did take one of the pears and ate it slowly, enjoying the taste, even though it was hard. After all, the chimps had eaten his granola bars.

Kriss got out his water bottle. The water was warm, but it was very satisfying. He let each chimp take a short drink, wiping the mouth of the bottle with a tissue when they were done. He remembered his toothbrush and took it out, willing to waste a bit of water to scrub his teeth.

The bigger chimp grunted, and Kriss looked at it. He watched as the chimp put its hand to its mouth, using its finger like a toothbrush, scrubbing back and forth across its big yellow-white teeth.

"Hey, *toothbrush*," Kriss said. "You guys really do know how to talk." He thought about the eating signs and the sign for tickling. "Wait a minute." He found the envelope on the ground and ripped it open. There were several official-looking letters and a booklet with the title: *Appendix A: Signing Vocabulary in Laboratory Chimpanzees*. The booklet was a twenty-five-page chart, with words and drawings.

After studying it a bit, Kriss had it figured out. The booklet listed 227 words that these chimps knew in sign language and showed how to make them. *Eat* was the eighth word on the list. *Tickle* was number seventeen. *Toothbrush* was thirty-five.

Kriss practiced those three signs with his back turned to the chimps. Then he turned around.

Toothbrush, he signed, his finger rubbing hard against his teeth.

The big chimp grabbed up Kriss's tooth-brush and held it in the air.

Kriss clapped and the little chimp imitated him. "Hey," said Kriss, "I think we're talking."

He signed *tickle* on the back of his hand, rapidly moving his finger across it. The chimps just stood there, watching. They did not seem to understand him. He made the sign larger, on his neck because the pamphlet had shown it there, too.

Still the chimps stared.

In desperation, Kriss ran his finger across his stomach.

At that, the littlest chimp flung itself at him, running its fingers across his stomach and under his arms. It tickled!

"I *know* we're talking," Kriss cried out before he started laughing. He was very ticklish, especially under the arms, and the chimp would not stop.

"Enough," Kriss cried at last, pushing the chimp away.

At his voice, the chimp stopped, rolled over on its back, and tickled its own stomach.

Kriss responded by getting on his hands and knees and tickled the chimp all over. At that, the bigger chimp joined in. They tickled one another until they were limp and exhausted and could only lie on the ground.

Kriss felt around and found the booklet. He looked up another word. Sitting up, he grabbed onto both his shoulders. *Hug,* he signed.

The chimps sat up and scrambled over to him. First the little chimp and then the larger one hugged him. Kriss smiled over their heads, out toward the empty sea. He would get them *all* back safely to L.A. He wasn't sure how. But he knew he could do it. For Ed the driver. And for the chimps. And partly for himself.

7/*Friday*

Kriss repacked, putting the food at the bottom of his knapsack in case the chimps decided to search for it. He tied the sleeping bag on firmly. Then he shouldered it all, keeping the compass in his pocket.

He found the sign for *go* and carefully made it several times at the chimps, both arms extended. He pointed down toward the cliff, since he thought they should start by checking out the remains of the road.

The chimps seemed to understand and ran on before him. They went on all fours, with feet flat on the ground and hands bent under so that they were walking on their knuckles. Kriss wondered if it hurt to walk that way. It certainly looked uncomfortable.

The chimps reached the edge of the ragged new cliff long before Kriss. He watched them standing and peering over the side.

"Wait for me," he called.

The bigger chimp looked up at him and stepped back from the cliff's edge. But the little one leaned even farther over, pointing at something. It jumped up and down excitedly. The cliffside began to crumble and fall away. The little chimp was carried over and out of sight, uttering a high-pitched scream.

On the edge, the big chimp stood and gave a long drawn out *"wraaah."* The hair of its shoulders and arms seemed to stand on end.

Kriss scrambled down the rest of the hill and ran as fast as he could, the pack banging against his back. He took the big chimp's hand and carefully led him along the edge, testing each footstep. At last they could

safely peek over. Far below, they could see
the remains of the lab van and beside it the
small, broken body of the little chimp.

"Wow," breathed Kriss, getting dizzy from
looking down. He backed away quickly,

pulling the big chimp with him, and sat on the ground. The chimp sat on his lap and put its arms around his neck. Without thinking, Kriss patted the chimp on the back. Tears streamed down Kriss's face. He wondered briefly why he was crying for the chimp when he hadn't cried for the driver of the van or all the people in the cars.

Kriss had no idea how long they sat that way. But the sun was high overhead when he pushed the chimp off his lap and stood up. His legs were cramped, and his back ached from the pack.

"Let's get out of here," he said to the chimp. Then he remembered the sign for *go* and used it, pointing back up the hill, but south, too. He knew that it would probably be closer to go north, to his grandmother's. But more than anything in the world he wanted to be home. And home was south, L.A. He reached out to the chimp, and hand in hand they headed up the hill.

At the edge of the woods, Kriss got out his compass. He used it often as they went deeper into the woods. He tried to locate their position on the map. It showed an enormous forest area, but he realized he couldn't be sure of their location until they crossed a road or came to a town. And, according to the map, towns, roads, and houses were few and far between.

They walked for hours, stopping only for a snack of apricots, granola bars, and water. Occasionally the chimp would leave, climbing a tree and going from branch to branch, tree to tree, in an easy swinging way that Kriss envied.

Several times the chimp disappeared and then reappeared carrying pieces of fruit, which it shared with Kriss. At first Kriss panicked when the chimp went off, calling out to it in screams. But the chimp always came back.

The third time, the chimp returned with pears and some berries that Kriss did not recognize and could not find in his booklet. Kriss ate only the pears. "I feel like Robinson Crusoe for real," he said to the chimp.

It stared back at him as if it understood what he was saying.

"Of course, if I'm Crusoe, then you," Kriss said, pointing to the monkey, "you are my companion, Friday."

The chimp mimicked his motions, pointing first to Kriss and then to its own chest.

Kriss laughed and slid out of his pack. Then he dug around in it until he found his copy of the book. He turned to a picture and pointed. "Me, Crusoe. You, Friday."

The chimp closed the book. It pointed to Kriss and then made eyeglasses with its hands, peering through them.

"Okay," Kriss said. "So I'm not Crusoe. I'm *Glasses* to you." He checked and, sure enough, *Glasses* was the sign the chimp had used. He signed it back, touching his chest first.

Satisfied, the chimp got up and swung back into the trees. It was gone for a long time, but now Kriss wasn't worried. It would return. He even made a joke for himself. "Friday will be back in a week's time." Somehow it almost made him laugh.

Friday was back in less than five minutes, chattering like crazy. It made the *go* sign in an eastern direction, and another sign Kriss could not figure out. Over and over it pointed *go* and finally leaped from the tree, grabbed Kriss by the hand, and pulled him.

"I don't know what you've seen, but you sure are in a hurry," Kriss said. He set his mouth and made a decision. This once, at least, he would follow the chimp. They couldn't get too lost as long as he had the compass and the map.

The chimp, seeing that Kriss was coming, ran on ahead. Kriss had to run, too, in order to keep up. Branches snapped in his face. He tripped over a root and had to catch hold of a tree trunk to stop from falling. More than once, limbs snagged on the backpack and he had to stop and work them loose.

Suddenly, the woods thinned. As he came to the top of a small hill, Kriss saw a clearing ahead. The chimp stood, pointing.

There was a house. A small cottage, really.

Kriss picked up the chimp and hugged it. Then he put it down. Hand in hand, they walked up the front steps to the door.

Kriss knocked. "Is anyone home?" he called out.

There was no answer.

He knocked again. Then he walked along the porch and peered through the window. He could see a living room with a sofa and some chairs and a rag rug on the floor. It was pretty dark inside.

"No one home," he said to Friday.

They went back and tried the door. It was locked. They walked around the house, trying all the windows and the back door, but everything was shut.

"This is an emergency, right?" Kriss asked the chimp. He took the silence for agreement and found a fist-sized rock. He walked over to a small window, brought his arm back to throw the rock, and then couldn't. It would be committing a crime. He put the rock down.

Friday picked up the rock and looked at it, then ran around the house on all fours. Kriss heard glass breaking and then a pattering inside the house. The doorknob turned and the door opened inward. Friday stood at the door grunting softly, gesturing with a hand.

"Well, since you're already in, and probably don't know your way around a house, I'd better come in, too," said Kriss. "Just to keep you out of mischief."

He walked in and looked around the quiet, darkened house. He found a light switch, but the lights didn't work.

"I have a bad feeling about this," Kriss said to the chimp. He found a telephone in the kitchen and tried to dial. After the third number, he realized the line was dead.

Kriss slumped in the chair and shook his head. "It's no good, Friday," he said. "I think the whole world has come to an end and we're the only two left alive."

8/A House for the Night

A gray fog began to close in on the house. Kriss stared out of the window. Just when he was the most scared, his stomach growled.

At the noise, Friday looked around and peeked under the chair.

Kriss began to giggle. It was hard to stay frightened with a growling stomach and a silly-looking chimp.

"Let's eat first and be scared later," Kriss announced. Then, remembering, he signed *eat*.

Kriss led the way to the refrigerator and opened it. The light was out. Inside were three rotting tomatoes and a quart of sour milk. Even the freezer was empty, with puddles of melted ice.

Kriss looked through the kitchen cupboards. He found a dozen cans of soup, some cans of fruit, and one of stewed tomatoes. In another drawer he found a can opener. He opened the beef vegetable soup before he realized that the stove was electric. They ate the soup uncooked, right from the can.

"That's not *too* bad," Kriss said, and opened a second, chicken noodle. Unheated, it was slimy. They did not finish it.

The chimp clapped its hands together and made the tickle sign on its belly. Kriss reached over and tickled it right on the spot, and the chimp rolled across the floor as if trying to get away. The game lasted until they bumped into the table and Kriss's glasses fell off and broke apart.

"Time out," Kriss said, standing up. In the

half-light, without his glasses, it seemed as if the fog had moved right into the house.

Kriss held one lens up to his right eye, his best eye, and looked around. He saw a small desk and opened its drawers. He found Scotch tape in the second drawer and taped the two pieces of his glasses together.

"Too dark to read. No working TV or radio. Guess it's time to go to bed," he said. He looked through the booklet to find the word *bed,* holding the papers up to the window to catch the last bit of light. He found bed, and it was easy to sign, a hand up by the side of his head.

Friday understood the first time, and imitated him. Then the chimp jumped onto the sofa.

"Not there," said Kriss, holding out his hand. He had seen a small room off the kitchen. It was a bedroom, only big enough for a double bunk bed and a dresser. Before Kriss could choose a bed, Friday had climbed to the top bunk and was happily arranging the pillow and blankets into a kind of nest.

Kriss shrugged and lay down on the lower bunk. Before he could remember to brush his teeth, he was asleep.

It was the chimp, not the daylight, that woke Kriss. Friday was cuddled by his side, patting Kriss's stomach and making the *eat* sign.

Kriss crawled out of bed and got his pack, dragging it into the bathroom. He brushed his teeth in the trickle of brown water that came from the tap. Then he went back and made both beds, pulling the hospital corners tight.

Breakfast was uncooked beef barley soup and canned peaches. Kriss washed everything carefully, dried the spoons, and put them away. But he found three sharp knives and some matches, which he put in his pack along with the remaining soup and the fruit cans. As an afterthought, he got out the spoons and took two. Then he wrote a note to the owners of the house:

"I borrowed three knives, some matches, and two spoons. I ate three cans of soup and fruit and have taken the rest. Here is $6. I hope that is enough. If not, please write to Kriss Pelleser, 6846 McLaren, Canoga Park, California 91304. P.S. I broke your window and will pay for that, too."

He left the note on the kitchen counter, next to the stove.

Kriss and Friday went out the front door, careful to lock it behind them, and started down the long, winding dirt driveway. It was full of holes and ruts.

The driveway went on for more than a mile, and they followed it in silence. At last it met a road that was so damaged, Kriss knew they would see no cars or trucks on it. He sat down by the roadside, and the chimp snuggled into his lap. Kriss liked that. It was more than just having a pet. It was almost like having a friend along.

Kriss checked the compass and then the map. He had no idea which road this was. But the compass pointed south. South to L.A. He was still a long, long way from home.

9/ *Human Contact*

Kriss and Friday traveled for three days without seeing anyone. They stayed close to the road, but huge gaps in the surface often forced them to walk many extra steps around the earthquake rubble. They saw a number of overturned cars. But after investigating one which had a dead driver and two dead passengers, Kriss left the cars alone. Twice helicopters flew overhead, but always when Kriss was in the woods. By the time he ran out to signal, they were too far away.

Kriss and Friday camped each night at the edge of the woods. The chimp preferred sleeping in a nest it built in the treetops. Because he was deathly afraid of bears, Kriss tried sleeping in a tree the first night. But there was no way he could get comfortable. He was so tired in the morning that he made up his mind to sleep curled at the foot of Friday's tree, with the three kitchen knives near at hand. He always woke to find the chimp snuggling close.

They ate two cans of soup a day, cold, because Kriss had forgotten to take a pot from the house. He had forgotten the can opener, too. But his jackknife had one, and after breaking three fingernails, he managed to get it open. Friday saw how it worked and opened it on one try. After that, opening cans became Friday's special job. All Kriss had to do was take out a can and hold it up, and Friday would find the jackknife.

Kriss rationed the food. There wasn't much. And he and Friday were constantly hungry, even though the chimp searched in the forest, often coming back with hard, wormy fruit, beetles, and leaves, which they divided up. Kriss checked everything in his plant book, but he left *all* the bugs and leaves to the chimp.

On the third evening, they heard voices coming from deeper in the woods. It almost sounded like a party.

"People," Kriss cried, and started toward the noise.

Friday hung back, whimpering, but Kriss plunged ahead. When he came to a clearing, Friday grabbed his hand and held on. They saw a large campfire with a group of men and women roasting meat. The smell was overpowering. Kriss's mouth began to water, but the chimp let out a small moan.

Kriss took off his glasses, rubbed them clean, and put them on again. He was about to call out to the strangers when he saw two dogs tied to stakes. He wondered if they were the cause of Friday's nervousness.

Just then, a man threw the bones of the meat to one dog who tore wildly into them, cracking off large pieces and eating the marrow. The man grabbed the chain of the second dog, a small spaniel, and pulled it toward the fire. It yelped and tried to get away.

"Let me do this one," a woman called. "I know it's hard on you. But I never did like dogs. It doesn't bother me." She stood up and went over to the man, taking a gun from his pocket. She held the gun to the dog's head. "Sorry, pooch. But we were too late to grab anything at the grocery store. And deliveries are a little slow during disasters. It's either you or us. So I guess it's you."

Kriss turned away quickly, his stomach heaving. He heard the shot and was sick.

Something touched his hand. He looked and it was Friday.

Eat? the chimp signed, hand to mouth.

Kriss gagged again and then bent over and picked up the chimp in his arms. Heedless of the sounds he made, he raced away into the woods, farther from the road and the people. He realized that if hungry people could eat dogs, they would certainly not hesitate to eat a chimpanzee.

He ran until he stumbled over a branch and they both went sprawling. The chimp was up in an instant, but Kriss was too out of breath to move. Night was closing in. He could not even see the hands of his compass.

Kriss signed *eat* to the chimp. He took off his pack and fished out the bag of apricots. He handed some to the chimp. *Eat, bed.*

Kriss fell asleep with his head on the knapsack, too tired even to open his sleeping bag. He did not know that overhead in a pine the chimpanzee had built a nest and was keeping a silent watch far into the night.

10/ Old Chris

Kriss and Friday stayed away from the road. The few times they thought they heard people, Kriss led them farther back into the woods. They ate berries, nuts, soup, and filled the water bottle in a clear stream they found.

Their biggest discovery, though, was a wild apple tree. The apples were small and hard. Many were rotten. They separated the apples into piles of good, not-so-good, and terrible. Kriss did the separating, and Friday climbed the tree to pick the apples near the top. They ate six apiece, put many more in

Kriss's pack, and were both up most of the night with sick stomachs. The chimp complained from its treetop nest, and Kriss groaned on the ground below.

But they survived. They were hungry, dirty, and often scared. Kriss's feet were blistered, his hands had poison ivy and his back hurt all the time. But they survived.

Kriss spent their frequent rest times reading and studying the sign language booklet. By the end of several days he had tried out the entire 227 words and had memorized many of them. A few—like *wagon, powder, harmonica*—he did not even try to learn. Friday helped him. When Kriss was slow to understand a sign, the chimp would sign it larger, with a great deal of patience. Once when Kriss really couldn't figure out what Friday wanted, the chimp bit him on the hand. It was not hard enough to break the skin, but it hurt. At that, Kriss slapped the chimp on the cheek. Friday scampered off and hid behind a tree until Kriss signed *sorry* five times. Friday came over and signed *sorry* back, looking quite sheepish. Then the monkey signed *me hug, me hug, me hug*. They hugged, and the incident was forgotten.

On the fifth day, while they were camped in a small clearing, Kriss woke with a hand on his shoulder. Eyes closed, he reached out sleepily to pat Friday. His fingers felt cloth. Kriss sat up and stared. He saw the blurred figure of a man bending over him. Kriss groped for his glasses and put them on.

An old man with a trimmed white beard and a ragged plaid wool shirt was kneeling by him.

"Hello, boy," the man said. "Been traveling alone long?"

"Alone? We . . . I . . ." Kriss stopped. He was suddenly aware that the old man was carrying no food but had a very large stick in one hand and a knife as big as a machete at his belt. Kriss gulped, tried to gather his courage, and stuttered. "A . . . alone. Yes. I'm alone. All alone." Hoping the chimp was awake and watching closely, Kriss made several quick motions with his hands. *Quiet. Go. Hurry. Go.*

There was a short flurry of leaves in the treetops and then silence.

Kriss relaxed and breathed deeply.

The old man shook his head. "Alone in the woods too long, boy. You start acting funny. Talk to yourself. Hear things. You nervous, boy?"

"Kriss. My name is Kriss." said Kriss.

"Well, isn't that something. That's my name, too. Christopher. The traveler's saint. Old Chris, they call me. The old man of the mountains to some. Live out in the woods in my own cabin. Built it myself. Used just nature's gifts—wood and stone. Wood and stone and Old Chris. Then the earth rumble drove me out. Sent down a ton of God's earth onto my roof. My well's gone. Windmill's gone. Vegetable patch disappeared down a crack." The old man shook his head and ran his one free hand through his hair. The hair was long, thick, straight, and pure white. It reached his shoulders.

Kriss felt he had to say something. "I'm sorry."

"Me, too, boy. Me, too. Then the Feder-ales came."

Kriss looked sideways at the old man. "Federales?"

"That's what I said, boy. Federales. The T-men. The CIA. Whatever they call them-selves these days. The Boys in Blue."

Kriss guessed. "You mean the police?"

"What I said, boy. In blue or in white or in gray or in black. They're all the same. They wanted to move me out. 'Rescue me' they said. *Rescue!* Wanted to put me in one of their little government boxes." The old man wiped his mouth with a surprisingly clean handkerchief that he brought out of his pocket. "They always want to put you in one of their government boxes. This one was a flying box with little whirling blades on top."

Kriss was beginning to get the hang of the old man's speech. "You mean a helicopter."

"Said it, didn't I, boy. *Helicopter,* that's just government language. Flying box is what it was. Wanted to take me away from my mountains. For my own good, they said. Said that back in 'sixty-eight, too. And 'forty-five. And 'thirty-nine." He tucked the handkerchief back in his pocket. "Wouldn't go though."

"Why not?" asked Kriss. "Were you scared?"

"Scared? Me? Was I scared in 'sixty-eight? Or 'forty-five? Or 'thirty-nine?" He smiled, "No, boy, I wasn't scared. I was terrified. Men weren't meant for boxes. And as for me, if God had wanted me to fly, I told them, he'd have given me a beak and a hunger for worms." He slapped his thigh and laughed at his own joke—a high, thin, wheezing. "And then I ran. I ran through the woods and those young buckoes could no more track me down than spit. Not a one of those box-trained bozos knows his way around a *real* forest. They only read about forests in books. Don't *know* the forests through their eyes and ears and nose and skin. That's knowing, boy. Course . . ." and the old man looked down at Kriss, his voice taking on a funny tone and his eyes getting slotted and sly, ". . . course, you must."

Kriss suddenly felt cold. "I must . . . what?" he asked.

Old Chris looked him over. "You must know the woods. You're awful young and awful far in, boy. With a pack. And by yourself. You *are* by yourself, aren't you? Are you lost? Or are you some kind of hero?"

Kriss could feel his stomach tighten. He thought suddenly about his father. What would *he* say. "I manage," said Kriss.

"Well, now, two of us might manage a bit better, don't you think?"

Kriss put his hand up to his glasses and slid them slowly back on his nose. He wasn't sure what to answer. He wasn't sure if the old man was offering help or asking for it. It was hard to tell if Old Chris was crazy, sly, or dangerous. "What do you mean?" he dared at last.

Old Chris didn't say a word, but reached down and pulled Kriss to his feet. The boy shrank back afraid, but the old man was terribly strong, stronger than he looked.

"Let go," Kriss cried out, striking at the old man's hands.

And suddenly there was a loud explosion of growls as a mass of fur leaped to the ground between them, barking and waving its arms. It was Friday, mouth wide open, teeth and gums bared.

"Friday, go away. Run. He'll kill you. He'll eat you. Run. Run," Kriss shrieked, trying desperately to make the monkey understand. But, in his desperation, he forgot to give any hand signs.

The old man dropped Kriss's hands and backed away from the angry chimp. He shook his head and began to laugh. "Don't that beat all," he said. "Eat him. Eat *him?* Boy, I haven't touched meat in forty-seven years, and I'm not about to start now. It'd take more than an earth rumble to turn Old Chris into a killer. A lot more, I can tell you that."

11/The Three of Them

Kriss and the old man sat back down on the ground, and the chimp sat a little away from them. At first Friday watched them, but as the two talked without hand signing, the chimp lost interest and began to wander around the clearing. From time to time it looked back at Kriss and gave a soft *hoo*. After a while, it gathered some leaves and the few dried berries it could find, popping them into its mouth.

Under a tree it found a clump of mushrooms. It picked them in one hand and sniffed carefully. Head to one side, Friday considered them. Then he trotted over on all fours to Kriss and dropped the mushrooms into his lap.

Kriss picked one up and signed *eat?*, making it a question by staring into the chimp's eyes.

Friday stared back, unblinking. *Eat.*

Kriss started to put one into his mouth, making a face because he hated mushrooms but was too hungry to protest.

"Wait," Old Chris cried, knocking his hand aside. "Don't eat those."

"Why not? Friday said they were for eating."

Old Chris shook his head. "Talks to you, does he? Well don't believe a word he says, boy. Don't trust anyone too much. Ever. Those particular mushrooms are poison. I ought to know. Lived on mushrooms for years. There's good ones and bad ones. And those are bad ones."

Kriss looked at Friday, and the chimp

hung its head down. It put its hands over its eyes and pushed its lips in and out several times, making a soft *hoo*.

"You lied to me, Friday. You *lied*." Kriss was shattered.

Friday tried to climb into Kriss's lap, but Kriss pushed him away signing *angry*.

"No, boy. Don't push him away. He's

sorry. And I doubt he understood what he could have done. He's just a bit jealous of Old Chris, I'd guess. Show him you're still friends. Go on." The old man nodded and Kriss relented.

Come, Kriss signed. *Hug.*

Friday gave him a hug, then signed *tickle*.

Kriss began to tickle the chimp. The old man joined them, and they rolled over and over in the grass.

At last they all sat up.

"Well, well, well," said Old Chris. "I guess he does talk. I heard tell of such. Reminds me of something I read once. That there's three kinds of intelligence in the encyclopedia: human intelligence, animal intelligence, and military intelligence. I think what we have here is a fourth kind."

Kriss smiled slowly. "A fourth kind. I like that." He rolled over onto his stomach and picked at a blade of grass. "You live around here, right?"

"Lived. In my own little house. Not thirty miles from here. Up in the woods. Living on my own," said the old man. "Now I guess I'm just existing. Things are bad, boy. Times are bad. Real bad. Why, I wouldn't even tell you some of the awful things I've seen this week. I thought I'd seen bad before. Was in the war and buried me a wife died of cancer. But what I've seen around here the last few days makes me ashamed of being human."

Kriss remembered clearly the scene at the campfire. He could hear the dog's cries echoing inside his head. "I know," he said softly. Then he sat up and looked at Old Chris. "But Friday and me, we're real hungry. And if there are places around here we could get some supplies . . . I've got about five dollars left. And I could call my folks. I've got to talk to them. Let them know I'm all right. Tell them . . ." his voice trailed off as he saw the old man shake his head.

"You don't understand, boy. All up and down the coast there were bad quakes. Some of Frisco and some of L.A. dropped into the ocean."

"L.A.! But that's where my mom and dad are. I *have* to call them. I *have* to." Kriss's voice was ragged.

"Boy, you aren't listening. Phones aren't working. People have been breaking into all the stores. Your money won't buy you anything. There's nothing to buy. That's what those bozos told me. The T-men, now, they drop supplies from their flying boxes once in a while."

"I've seen them," Kriss said, nodding. "At least, I've seen some helicopters. But they weren't dropping anything."

"Might have been scouts," said the old man. "But, boy, it's going to be weeks, months even, before things get straightened out."

"I didn't know . . ." Kriss began, but the

old man didn't hear him and kept talking.

"It's war, you know. War between us humans and the earth we've hurt for so long."

"But there must be *something* left," Kriss cried, his voice cracking. "Something more than berries and bad mushrooms."

"I don't know," the old man said.

Kriss interrupted. "What about a drug store? Or a dime store? Or a pet store? There might be food there. For us. Or for Friday."

"Well now," Old Chris mused, scratching his head. The chimp, who had lost interest in the conversation, saw the old man scratching and walked over and began grooming the long white shoulder-length hair. "There used to be a pet store at one of the little malls. Went there once for a book about squirrels. Trying to raise a nest of them. Being a mother to squirrels isn't easy! Books are good friends. Better than people." He was patting the chimp on the head, losing the thread of his talk.

"The pet store," Kriss pressed.

"Oh yes," Old Chris picked up again. "It's maybe five miles. Not more. Two roads to cross. But a lot of woods, too."

"Let's go," said Kriss.

The old man carried the sleeping bag and Kriss the backpack. They shared three hard apples on the way, the last ones Kriss had. There was only one can of soup left, and he was saving it for their evening meal.

12 / The Pet Store

The pet store was in a small tree-shaded mall that included two dress shops, a furniture store, a shoe store, and a gift shop. Many of the windows in the mall were broken, and most of the trees were lying on their sides as if their root systems had been too new or too weak to hold them to the earth. The parking lot and the sidewalks leading to the mall were a jumble of cement. Great cracks, like giant spider webs, ran up and down the sides of the buildings. Packing cartons, boxes, and paper bags lay in the streets, signs that the stores had been looted. The mall was completely deserted. Yet it made Kriss think of home. His eyes and throat suddenly hurt. He blinked quickly to keep back tears.

Old Chris pointed to the pet store. "Boxes. Putting beasts in boxes. It may not be pretty in there. If there are any small animals left, they may all be dead or dying. They won't have been fed for a week."

"Then we *have* to go in," said Kriss. "At least to feed them. Or set them free."

"We'll see, boy," the old man said. "We'll see."

They stood another fifteen minutes staring around the mall, alert for the sight or sound of other people. Kriss had to sign *lie down* to Friday three times before the chimp quieted.

At last, sure that no one else was near, the three edged toward the rear of the buildings. It was a safer route. They found the back of the pet store unlocked.

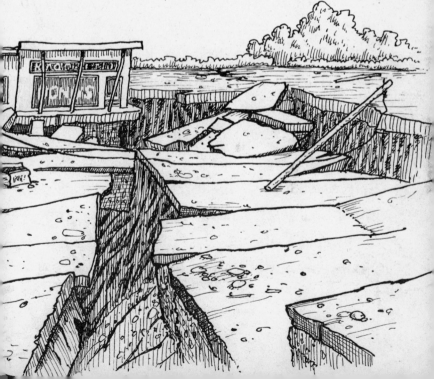

"I'll go in first, boy," said Old Chris. "And I'll let you know if everything is all right."

Kriss started to protest, but he was secretly relieved. "Friday and I will stand guard," he said.

The old man pulled open the door and slipped inside. Kriss could hear him pushing things around. Then there was a silence.

"Everything all right?" Kriss called out in a harsh whisper, his mouth close to the door. Beside him, the chimp was rocking nervously side to side.

"Come on," the old man called out at last. "I need your help with something. But hold your nose. It's bad."

Kriss signed *sit* to Friday and, taking a deep breath, went into the store.

It was shadowy inside. Boxes and cages were spilled everywhere. Kriss had to climb over several shattered glass cases. Fish tanks, leaking water through cracks, were everywhere. Kriss tripped over a metal cage and its door swung wide. He wondered what had been inside. Maybe nothing.

"Over here," Old Chris called.

Kriss turned toward his voice and saw the old man bent over a large cage on the floor. In it was a small starved-looking chimp. The chimp was whimpering softly.

"Can't see well enough in this light. I think the door jammed when the cage fell," said Old Chris.

Kriss stared through his glasses, took them off, and rubbed the lenses on his shirt. Putting them on again, he squinted. "Maybe we should just take the whole cage outside and open it there."

"It's pretty heavy," said Old Chris. "I'm having trouble lifting it. But the two of us together should be able to manage."

Kriss helped. It *was* heavy. As he lifted, he heard a strange, slithering sound behind the old man. Kriss looked up. Something was slowly moving toward them, flowing along the floor like a long, dark wave.

"What is that?" asked the old man, turning around.

Even in the half-light of the room, Kriss knew what it was. "A snake," he breathed. "A huge snake."

Old Chris saw it then, too. "A boa, boy. A big one, too. Pet stores sometimes carry them. They put them all in boxes. But that snake doesn't know us. It might be hungry. I'll keep it busy, distract it while you slide this cage out of here. Go, boy. Or that snake will try for a chimp dinner and maybe a boy for dessert."

Kriss dragged the heavy metal cage behind him. When he reached the back door he pushed it open with his rear and pulled the cage out. The little chimp whimpered and Friday screamed. Kriss fell on the ground. Then he crawled on his hands and knees back to the door. He could hear the awful slithering in the dark. What if the snake came out and chased him? He'd run, he knew he'd run. He'd leave Friday and Old Chris and the little chimp behind. Kriss knew he would because *nothing* scared him as much as a snake. Even snake pictures made him feel queasy. He leaned his shoulder against the door and it slammed shut. But even with the door closed, he thought he could still hear the snake sliding, sliding across the pet store floor.

13/Heroes Don't Cry

In the awful hush that followed the slamming door, Kriss could feel, then hear, his heart thudding. He began to cry, awful gulping sobs that seemed to split the air.

Over and over he could hear himself saying the words, "Heroes don't cry. Heroes don't cry." But he could not stop crying.

Friday crept over to him and patted his hand gently. Then the monkey made a sign that Kriss only partly recognized. Kriss took off his glasses, wiped his eyes, and put the glasses back on. The sign was *man* combined with one he had never seen before. The chimp became nervous and made the sign again, hand pulling at its chin.

And then Kriss knew. Friday had made up the sign, and it looked like a beard. *Man-beard.* Friday meant Old Chris, the man with the beard. Friday understood that something was wrong inside the building. And Kriss knew he could not let either the old man or the chimp down.

He took a deep breath, set his jaw, and put his hand on the doorknob. He had to help get Old Chris out. Even if it meant fighting the snake. *The snake!* Thinking about it made the awful slithering sound begin again in his head.

"I—am—not—a—hero!" he screamed at the top of his lungs. The tears started down again, but he yanked the door open and looked in.

There was a movement in the shadows. A slow, sliding sound. Kriss's voice squeaked out, "Chris? Old Chris?"

Something fell with a terrible crash. Kriss backed away from the door, tripped, and went down. His glasses fell off. Wildly, he searched in the dirt until he found them. One lens was gone, the other cracked. He could barely see. When he looked up, something large was coming out the door toward him.

"Come on, boy. Let's get away from this box." It was the old man. He was breathing heavily and his hand was clutching his chest.

They shut the door together.

Kriss turned to the old man. "Are you . . . ? Did you . . . ? You're safe!" he cried out and to his shame felt the tears starting down again. He hugged Old Chris and felt the rough tickle of the old man's beard on the top of his head.

"I think," Old Chris began, stopped, then started again. "I think the snake's heart wasn't in the chase. Too many easy days eating hamsters and white mice."

Kriss looked up at him. "Did you have to, you know. Use your knife?" Kriss looked at the machete, which was still in the old man's belt.

"Me? I told you, I haven't touched meat in thirty-seven years," said Old Chris laughing and then suddenly groaning.

"*Forty*-seven you said," Kriss corrected.

The old man shrugged and smiled quickly.

"But what if the snake had gotten you. I mean, what if he had caught you and was squeezing you and squeezing you and you might have died and . . . ?"

The old man smiled again. "Then I would have been in what we used to call a *moral di-lemma,*" he said. He looked intently at Kriss. "Let's get that little one out of the cage and us out of here. I think I need to lie down somewhere and rest. Somewhere far away from that boa."

The old man was clearly in pain. He often rubbed his chest and moaned softly. They could go no farther than the wood's edge carrying the sleeping bag, backpack, and the little chimp.

"That's a nice little lady chimp for your gentleman there," said the old man, once he was lying down.

Kriss was embarrassed to admit that he had never thought about Friday's sex.

"Adam and Eve like," Old Chris continued. He put his hand to his chest and said,

"I'm a little better now, I think." But he didn't make any move to get up, not right away.

They managed to nurse the little chimp back to health, with Kriss and Friday doing most of the fetching and carrying. Old Chris lay around a lot and gave directions.

They named the little chimp Eve. And with water and fruit and even some bird's eggs that Friday found, they fattened her up. Inside of days, she was romping with Friday and had even learned to sign *tickle, water, hug, eat.* It was Friday who took the time to teach her. Kriss was too busy worrying about the old man.

They moved through the woods much more slowly now. Old Chris needed frequent rests. Often he asked Kriss to massage his chest and his left arm. He joked about how the boa had scared all the energy out of him.

"Bet you weren't *really* scared," Kriss said

to him, one night when they were camped in a clearing. They had finished a meal of scrambled bird's eggs and wild onions cooked over a tiny fire. Old Chris felt a small fire for a few minutes would do no harm. He showed Kriss how to use an old soup tin as a pot.

"Not scared?" the old man said. "I was so scared in there, I couldn't see. My eyes filled up with tears 'til that snake looked like he was swimming across the ocean toward me."

"But you're a hero," said Kriss. "Heroes don't cry."

"Who says, boy? Of course heroes cry. Everybody cries," the old man said. "But not everybody admits it. I cried in the war when my buddies died. I cried when I buried my wife, Not for them. No, I didn't cry for them. Cried for me, 'cause I was still there, caring about them. People in the war called *me* a hero. Hero! What did they know? A hero, now, that's just someone who makes a hard choice. And not even always the right choice, mind you." He held his left arm over his chest and rubbed it with his right. Then, looking exhausted, he closed his eyes and seemed to sleep.

Kriss sat and stared at the fire through his broken glasses. The flames took on a strange red magic and he was almost hypnotized by them. At last he got up and stomped out the fire.

The two chimps stood up. Eve, who always asked the old man for a hug before sleeping, went over to him. She put her head on his chest for a second, as if listening for a heartbeat. Then she straightened up and chattered excitedly at Kriss.

Friday, alarmed, went over to investigate. Then he turned and signed, *Come. Man-beard* . . . not able to sign the proper words he beat the ground with his hands. At last he signed *sleep,* hitting his own hands away as if denying this was, indeed, a proper sleep.

Kriss fearfully went over to the old man and tried to wake him. Old Chris moaned faintly but did not open his eyes.

"Please, Old Chris, please," Kriss begged. "Wake up. Please."

The old man slept on, a sleep of sickness, a kind of coma.

Eve took the old man's hand and kissed it. Friday signed *good-bye* and began to rock back and forth.

"No!" shouted Kriss. "No. It's not good-bye. I won't let it be. I won't."

14/ Some Kind of Hero

Kriss's first thought was to keep the old man as warm as possible. Though the days were nice enough, the northern California nights were cool and foggy. He unrolled his sleeping bag, unzipped it, and pushed the old man gently onto it, wrapping the bag around him.

Then Kriss decided to start another fire. A big blaze. He no longer cared if the fire was seen by other people. He needed to keep Old Chris warm. The chimps could stay in the treetops. For now, they would have to take care of themselves.

With the last of the matches, Kriss started

the fire. Then he moved the old man as close to it as he dared. He took out the water bottle in case Old Chris woke up. The only time he left the old man's side was to get more wood.

For two hours, the roar of the fire and the old man's rattling breathing were the only sounds Kriss heard. The fire danced and sparkled through the single lens of his broken glasses like a crazy kaleidoscope. Kriss kept himself awake imagining what would happen if the old man died. Would he be able to dig a grave? Make a cross? Would he ever be able to find his way back to this place and see that there was a real headstone on Old Chris's grave? After burying the old man in his imagination, Kriss began to wonder what he would do in the morning if Old Chris were still alive. It was obvious he needed a doctor. Could he be carried to the road? Dragged Indian-style in a sled made of sticks and string? Could the chimps help?

He got up and cut down a big tree limb with the machete. Cross or sled, he could use it for either. He sat down again by Old Chris's side and began to trim the branch. He never felt sleepy, but he fell asleep, the tree limb across his lap. He woke only when dawn began chasing strands of fog across the almost-dead fire. The two chimps were beside him, pulling on his arm.

Kriss woke, startled. He pushed the limb off his lap and arched his back. He was stiffer than he had ever been. Both legs were asleep. He had to stomp around to wake them. Then he went to check on Old Chris. The old man was still alive, breathing heavily, mumbling. Kriss put more branches on the fire and bent over to blow on the embers. The leaves caught, and the fire crackled to life again.

The two chimps hauled something over to the fire and dropped it in. It was the big limb.

"No, stop. That's not for the fire," Kriss

yelled. He ran at them and they backed away in fear. When Kriss realized they had only been trying to help, he squatted down and immediately signed *sorry*. But the noise of his own yelling had kept him from hearing

another noise. The chimps spotted it first and
looked up. Overhead, high above them, a
helicopter was making a pass. It probably
had seen the smoke from the fire and was
coming to check. With the sun behind it, the

copter looked like a great winged creature. "An angel," Kriss thought, and then just as quickly added, "or a vulture."

He looked at the old man and then at the chimps. He thought about his own parents and his grandmother. Then he made up his mind. He took off his shirt and T-shirt and wrapped the T-shirt around the top of the stick, plunging it into the fire. He waved it like a signal torch, yelling up at the copter: "Here. Down here. Help us. Over here."

The copter circled the clearing once and began its descent, but Kriss ignored it. He turned instead to the chimps who were standing together. He held out his jackknife to them.

Take, he signed. *Run. Climb. Time go.* Then before they could move, he gave them each a hug and spoke out loud. "I don't know the sign, but remember me. Remember . . ." and then he signed *glasses, man-beard.* He put his hand over his heart. It wasn't any sign in the book, but he hoped the chimps would understand. He meant "Remember me. In your heart." Then his eyes began to fill with tears and he signed *hurry, go.* He pushed them away. But all the while he shielded them from the copter with his body. He had to sign *hurry, go* three times more before they would leave.

They went as if getting ready to play another run-tickle game. Perhaps they thought that was all it was. He would never know.

Kriss walked back to the fire and saw that Old Chris was awake at last, watching him. He squatted down and waited until the pilot and co-pilot came over to them. Then he stood.

"My name is Kriss Pelleser," he said, wondering that his voice was so calm when he knew they could see he had been crying. "I'm from L.A. and I'm lost. I want to go home." He pushed the broken glasses back on his nose and pointed to the old man. "He's my friend and he's sick and he doesn't like being boxed up. Also he's a little bit afraid of flying. But it's okay. I'll hold his hand."

The pilot nodded and knelt by Old Chris, checking his pulse. The co-pilot went back for a stretcher. They lifted him gently onto the canvas.

Kriss took a minute to put on his shirt and put out the fire. Then he picked up his sleeping bag and backpack and trotted after them.

He heard the co-pilot saying "Stuffy little kid, ain't he. Looks and sounds like a school teacher. It's a wonder he wasn't eaten by bears." Kriss just bit his lip and managed a smile. He walked by the stretcher's side.

The old man reached out and took Kriss's hand in his. "Actually, this boy's some kind of hero," he said. "But I'm not sure you two box-bred bozos would understand."

"Bozos," grumbled the co-pilot.

The pilot just smiled.

Kriss squeezed the old man's hand and didn't even mind that new tears were making new trails of dirt down his face.

He settled himself in the copter next to the stretcher. Then he looked out the window. The clearing suddenly seemed very small. As the copter rose, the clearing got smaller still.

Beyond the smoky remains of the fire, by the wood's edge, Kriss thought he saw a bit of movement. Two tiny dark figures waving good-bye. But with only one lens in his eyeglasses, there was no way he could be sure. He squeezed the old man's hand once. "I'll get you back to the woods real soon," he promised.

"You know, boy," said Old Chris, "I believe you will."

A Note to the Reader

The story of Kriss Pelleser and Friday is not a true one, but scientists have been working with chimps and gorillas for several years, teaching them a basic language of hand signs. The hand signs are based on the American Sign Language, which was developed for deaf people. Scientists report that several of the animals have almost two hundred words in their signing vocabulary. Washoe, the first chimp to be taught sign, has begun teaching it to her adopted child.

There is as yet no agreement among scientists as to what this all means. Some claim that animals—chimps and gorillas in this case—are capable of true language. Others feel the animals merely repeat what they have been taught and cannot invent sentences, which is the true test of language.

But even though scientists may disagree about the talking chimps, they all agree that there is a real possibility that one day California will have a different coastline than the one it has today.

Some of Friday's Vocabulary

hug

eat

go

toothbrush

come

tickle

beard

glasses

water

good-bye

run

hurry